BROKEN WING

From the series

Fairies of Aurora Village.

BOOK 1

Written by

Maureen Larter

Illustrations by Annie Gabriel

This book is for my grandchildren
And all the grandchildren across the world.

CONTENTS

First printed in 2012 by Maureen Larter, Wingham
Illustrations by Annie Gabriel 2010

ISBN 978-0-9873500-3-9

A hardcopy record is held at the
'National Library of Australia' in
Canberra N.S.W. Australia.
(bound by Creative Leather Binding,
Taree, N.S.W. Australia)

Website: ebooksbymaureenlarter.com
Facebook: facebook.com/ebooksbymaureenlarter
Twitter: @maureenlarter
Email: maureenlarter@gmail.com

CHAPTER 1

The Picnic

Granny Flannigan loved her beautiful acreage in the middle of the tropical rainforest of North Queensland. Her back yard was wild and natural. On the back verandah of her home, several pot plants flourished. Nearby she had placed a comfy lounge, where she often sat and contemplated the beauty around her.

Living here was her idea of bliss. She would quietly walk around her property and marvel at the gorgeous native plants, and wish that more people could enjoy her abundant environment.

She knew she was lucky. She realised that through necessity most people had lost the wonder of nature as they lived their life bound up in family, jobs and bills.

What she *didn't* know was that fairies lived at the bottom of her garden! And, to be honest, that's the way the fairy people of Aurora village liked it.

Ruled over by Queen Isabella, the village was a remote, peaceful place hidden deep within the luscious rainforests at the back of Granny's property. The forest was truly bountiful and there were plenty of resources for their needs.

Petula was a dainty little girl fairy, about the same age as a ten-year-old human child. Just like Granny, she loved living in this beautiful spot. She would flit around from one place to the next, smiling and chatting with the other folk in the village. After school had finished, she would often visit her friends. Her brother, Denbo, kept telling her she should help her mother more, but Petula just laughed and told him he should help instead.

Today was one of those days when nobody should stay inside. The sun was shining, and a cool breeze stirred the leaves of the trees towering above the village. The flowers seemed more brilliantly coloured and the birds were singing much more tunefully. Petula decided it was the perfect time to have a picnic with her friends.

Her mother made up a lovely hamper of food for her and as the basket was heavy they asked Denbo to put it on their cart. With the help of their trained grasshopper Springer, harnessed to the cart, Denbo proceeded to drive over to the clearing where they were going to have their feast.

Her friends, Daisy and Pansy, lived over the other side of

the village, so Petula set out happily to visit them. She gave a cheery wave to her mother, and called over her shoulder to her brother.

"Won't be long. I'll go and get my friends. See you soon." And then she disappeared toward her friends' house.

She flew through the village, greeting many of the elfin people as she went. Every now and then, she bent to smell a flower, or land on a swaying branch of a tree and look at the busy native bees collecting the nectar to take back to their hive.

She liked the hum of the tiny insects and, as they didn't sting like the big bees, she had a game with two of them, zigzagging around them and calling them names. Her tinkling laughter made several of the older fairies look up at her and smile. She waved to them, then continued on her way, singing a sweet song.

She saw Mistress Gondola's shop. It had a window full of brightly coloured spider web material and she often went there with her mother to get material for their new dresses. Raeff, Denbo's friend, was there helping Mistress Gondola move some of the heavy rolls of cloth. He saw Petula and gave her a cheeky smile. She had stopped and was hovering near the shop staring at him with her large blue eyes. He was very handsome! She flew backwards as she continued to look at Raeff.

"Watch where you're going, Petula!"

Petula jumped, then apologised humbly to Prion, the Queen's artist. She had nearly bumped into him and she was a little afraid and in awe of the great man. Prion was so involved with thinking and planning his next painting, that he didn't really notice Petula, or her apology, very much at all. He strode into Mistress Gondola's shop.

"Hello, Sylvettia," he said to Mistress Gondola. "I'm looking for some beautiful…."

His voice faded into the distance as Petula continued on her journey. Not far away, she saw an old gnome sitting in the sun, his head nodding as he snoozed.

"Hello, Toby," she called and waved to the grizzled old gnome who sat enjoying the sun's warmth. He was reclining on the protruding root of the tree above his home. Toby looked up at Petula, his long hat bobbing over his eyes as he awoke with a start, trying to look as if he had just been thinking. He pushed the hat out of his way and grinned at her. Petula was pleased, because he seldom smiled.

"Where are you off to?" he asked.

Petula daintily alighted next to him and smiled up into his crinkled face.

"I'm going to Pansy and Daisy's place and we're all going on a picnic. Denbo is taking our food on his cart with Springer, to the little glen near the creek."

Toby patted her hand.

"Go and have a lovely day, " he said. "Be careful." Then he leant back on the tree and once again closed his eyes.

It wasn't long before Petula was gliding down to a little tidy cottage, hidden near a small red cedar sapling, in which Pansy and Daisy lived.

Daisy and Pansy were delighted to see her and, after asking permission to go with Petula, they all chatted and laughed merrily as they fluttered off to meet Denbo.

The small clearing they had picked for their picnic was nestled amongst the ferns, near a small stream. Denbo arrived almost at the same time as the three girls and they unpacked the cart.

“I’ll see you later, girls,” he said as he jumped up onto the empty cart. “I’m off to see Raeff for the day. Go, Springer!” With that he quickly disappeared into the forest.

Daisy began to dish out the food that Petula’s mother had packed into the hamper. There were home-made honey biscuits, several lillypilly berries, a bottle of passionfruit juice and some delicious banana sandwiches. At the same time, Pansy and Petula flew around the area, searching out the flowers and native orchids that grew nearby.

"Careful, girls," a deep voice croaked, causing the fairies to jump with surprise.

"Ooh, Mr Jumper, you did scare us," Pansy looked at the large green tree frog sitting quietly on a leaf near the water. "Is there anything the matter?" she asked.

The green frog cleared his throat and looked around with a furtive air.

"Mr Wrinkle, the big cane toad, is not well today, and it's best if you keep out of his way. You know how vicious he can be. He gets so agitated that the poison sacs on his head ooze. He's over in the next clearing – please be extra careful!"

The girls were most grateful to Mr Jumper and they promised to steer clear of Mr Wrinkle, as they had seen him when he was angry, and were quite frightened of him.

After all the lovely food was finished, the girls were tired. They curled up in the shade and tried to have a quiet time, playing a game of 'I Spy'.

"I spy with my little eye, something beginning with...." Pansy looked around for a little while as she tried to think of something clever. She saw a mosquito hovering over the water and decided that would be a good idea. “With ‘M’” she finished with a rush.

Petula and Daisy looked and looked, but the little clearing was warm and the girls were full of delicious food and they were very drowsy.

Daisy was the first to speak. “It’s no good. I just can’t concentrate. The afternoon is getting hot and the cicadas are getting too noisy!”

“Mmm,” Petula agreed lazily. “I’m so full I think I would like to go to sleep.”

Daisy laughed, looking at Petula as her eyes almost closed.

“Not a chance,” she said. “The cicadas are just deafening. I think we ought to pack up and go home.” As she spoke she began to clean the leaves they had used as plates and lifted the lid of the hamper to put away the cups and the last of the food.

Daisy and Pansy were soon ready and with a smile and a wave they were flying off in the direction of their own homes

CHAPTER 2

The Mantis.

Not far away, Petula saw the most beautiful tree that was covered in blossoms. She was enthralled by the sight, and she flew into the branches and sat on a small branch breathing in the heady aroma of the native frangipani flowers. A few of the Australian wild bees were gathering the pollen and the humming of their wings combined with the perfume of the flowers and the full stomach of food she had enjoyed, caused Petula to begin to doze.

Suddenly a strange feeling that she was being watched awakened her. She opened her eyes and looked around.

Not more than a jump away, was a large Praying Mantis, swaying in the breeze as he stared at her intently. Petula could almost see the danger vibrating in the air as the Mantis seemed to shrink back ready to strike.

There was no time to think and Petula knew she had to get away.

With a huge jump, she launched herself into the empty space above her and cried out in shock. A small twig had caught her wing, and she fell, hanging in mid-air. The Praying Mantis moved and, in her desperate attempt to escape, she felt the wing tear. She fell to the ground below, her one good wing fluttering so that she was lucky to land reasonably softly.

There was no way she could fly home, and she sat on a small patch of lichen and cried and cried. She felt relief at her escape, but it was mingled with fear, sadness and the realisation that she was wounded. Now she had to get home and, as she was so used to flying, it seemed an almost impossible distance to walk.

After a little while, she calmed down and was able to look around and try and work out where she was. She looked at her wing and almost began sobbing again. It hung from her shoulder blade, useless. It was torn through the centre.

She decided it was no use feeling sorry for herself, she would just have to start walking.

A bird fluttered from branch to branch above her as she dejectedly trudged home. Finally, the bird came down to a low branch startling Petula when it spoke.

“What’s wrong?” it asked.

Petula was so stunned that she began to cry again.

“Don’t cry!” the bird said almost crossly. “How can I help you if you won’t tell me what’s wrong!”

“I..I.. bbbro,” but she got no further as she sat down with a plonk on the ground and sobbed again.

The bird became quite agitated. It hopped from one leg to the other, flapping its white wings and fluffing up the feathers on its plump little chest.

“OK!! Enough!!” The bird screeched. “Listen to me. If I can fly all the way from Papua New Guinea and arrive here at Mrs Flannigan’s small patch of glorious rainforest, then you can tell me what’s wrong!”

Petula had by now stopped crying and was looking at the bird with awe. The bird cooed then stopped still for a moment. He looked at Petula with his dark eyes, then said, quietly. “By the way, my name is Walter!”

Petula almost smiled. “What sort of bird are you? She asked. “I haven’t seen any others like you before.”

“Well,” and the bird puffed out his chest even more. “I’m a Torresian Imperial Pigeon and there are not many of us about. In about 1960 two lovely people stopped hunters from shooting my friends, and now there are many more than there used to be, but now we have trouble finding some rainforest to stay in when we come over here. Thank goodness for Granny Flannigan!”

Petula was amazed. It was wonderful to know that the birds, like Walter, who lived in another country for part of their lives, knew about the wonderful patch of rainforest at the back of Granny Flannigans’.

She forgot her troubles because she was so interested in the story Wally was telling her. She was talking happily with Wally and he didn’t seem to mind that she had shortened his name. He said it was a very Australian thing to do! She finally told him what had happened and why she was upset when he first saw her.

She began to shake when she described the feeling of fear when she was staring into the face of the Praying Mantis. She showed him the torn wing and he was most comforting

“Never mind,” said Wally, “climb on my back and I’ll fly

you home. After the long trip I've just done, this will be easy - as you Aussies say - a piece of cake!'

The trip home went by in a flash. Petula was thrilled to be a rider on Wallys' back. She was able to look around at the countryside from a new viewpoint, and she was amazed at all the things that she could see. When she was flying around normally, she never went as high as Wally could go – and she didn't fly nearly as fast.

At one stage she almost felt afraid as they flew above the treetops and she held on to Wallys' feathers so tightly that he had to ask her to relax.

"Please don't hold on so tightly," he said. "It feels as if my feathers might get pulled so much that they will fall out!"

"Oh! Sorry!" Petula said, letting her hands loosen their hold on Wallys' feathers.

It didn't take long before they arrived at Petula's home and Wally landed in front of the neat little garden, scattering several fallen leaves as he fluttered to a stop. Petula carefully got down onto the ground outside the pretty little cottage just as her mother came out of the door.

Almost at once, Petula burst into tears again. Wally put a wing around her and her mother rushed to her side.

"What's wrong?" she asked, then turned to the bird and looked him up and down. "And who are you, and what are you doing with my daughter?"

The bird squinted at Petulas' mother, but then told her his name and began to tell her his story. She patted his wing, and interrupted him.

"I think that's wonderful, but you must tell me all about it later," she said. Wally nodded. Petulas' mother continued. "First, we must see to Petula." She hugged a still sobbing Petula and spoke softly to her daughter.

"Come on, my love, tell me what's wrong."

Petula finally showed her mother the broken and useless wing drooping from her shoulders and stammered out the scare that she had had when she had seen the Praying Mantis.

"Come on, smile, my love," her mother hugged her even tighter. "I can fix that. All I need is some nice strong webbing, and you'll be as good as new!" Petula gave her a watery smile and Wally looked pleased too.

"Now," Petula's mother took a deep breath. "Let's get organised." She looked at Wally. "Thank you for your help," she said to him. "I don't know what we would have done without you. Please accept my gratitude and stay for some food."

Wally puffed out his chest with pride and said, with dignity, "It was an honour to look after Petula. Is there anything else I can do before I go back to my friends in the trees at the back of the property here?"

"Oh! How kind!" Petulas' mother exclaimed. She tried to give Wally a hug, but he gruffly strutted away a little. "Before you go," she said to him when she realised that she was embarrassing him. "Perhaps you could find Denbo, Petula's brother. He will have to go and get me some good strong web. If he can find a bird spider, that would be ideal!"

Wally visibly shuddered.

"Oh, I'm sorry!" Petulas' mother hurriedly explained. "That's just their name. You are perfectly safe! They only rarely catch birds, and then only very small ones!"

Wally relaxed again, then agreed to find Denbo for them.

CHAPTER 3

Off to find the bird spider.

Just as he did so, Denbo came sauntering along the little pathway towards the base of the Eucalypt tree where Petula and her family lived.

"Ah!' there you are, Denbo!"

Denbo stopped and looked with astonishment at Wally.

"My goodness," he said, seeing Petula and his mother talking to the large bird. "What's happened?"

So of course they had to tell him!

They all started talking to him at the same time, until he held up his hand in mock surrender. "Whoa!" he exclaimed. "One at a time, please!"

He eventually understood what had happened, even though he had to stop them several times and ask questions. The story got a little confused when Wally started to add in his story of travelling from overseas and Petula kept having a cry and everyone had to give her some comfort.

Finally, after examining Petulas broken wing and listening to his Mother telling him that she needed a special type of strong web to fix it, Denbo realised that he would have to go and get it for her.

He decided to take his best friend, Raeff, as a companion. He wasn't going to admit that he was a little frightened of the bird spider. He knew he could easily become entangled in the strong web and become a tasty morsel if he wasn't careful. With Raeff along, he would have to listen to lots of jokes and it would take his mind off the fear.

That very afternoon, after gathering together some food to eat on the journey, the two elves began their journey.

It wasn't long before both the elves were hungry so they stopped under a pretty lomandra, with its swaying, strappy leaves. The air was cool and less humid underneath the tall grass. They were both grateful for the rest.

"Why does everyone want us to do all these errands?' groaned Raeff. "We always seem to get called to do them. Why didn't they ask Jacoby or Larimar this time?"

Denbo laughed.

"Can you imagine Jac doing anything at all? And Lari is such a small fellow, he'd probably get lost in the grass!"

Raeff laughed too, nodding his head in agreement.

Just as he began to speak, they heard voices, and from over the nearby ridge appeared two elves, talking and laughing. They each had a backpack over their shoulders, and wore gaily coloured hats and scarves.

"They must be around here somewhere," said one of the elves, looking around as he spoke.

"I know, Geri," said the other elf. "I'm sure we can help them. I wish they had asked before they left."

"Hi! Lari," called Denbo, glancing at Raeff and lifting his eyebrows with surprise. "We're over here."

Geriron and Larimar came over, smiling broadly. "We've come to help!" they said together, sitting down under the thin leaves of the lomandra with Raeff and Denbo.

Raeff and Denbo grinned.

"At least you didn't bring Jac," said Raeff. "He can be more trouble than he's worth!"

Lari looked at Geri and sighed.

"He really wanted to come, and we had to sneak off so he wouldn't follow," Lari admitted.

"I wouldn't be surprised if he turns up later, anyway," Geri added.

The boys searched in their backpacks and pulled out their lunch. For several minutes there was silence as everyone thought about Jac and they ate their food.

Suddenly an awful racket sounded very close by. They sprang to their feet in horror and began to run towards the sound - well, everyone except Lari - who ran to hide!

Denbo skidded to a halt just short of a clump of native orchids. He held up his hand to stop the other elves.

"Ssh! Look!" he pointed up into the canopy of trees a short way away.

Two cockatoos were shouting at one another. Each one was fluffed up, with wings outstretched and crests raised. Their squawking and squabbling was so loud, that everything else around seemed silent in comparison.

Their fluttering dislodged leaves and several smallish twigs which rained down on the small band of elves below.

Lari crept up towards the group. They were all staring up at the birds and didn't notice him. As the debris from the skirmish above reached them, they broke rank and rushed for cover.

The only one who didn't, of course, was Lari.

A larger twig hit him on the head and he collapsed in a little heap on the forest floor as the birds kept up their argument and more litter fell from above.

Finally, still squabbling, the cockatoos flew off and Denbo, Raeff and Geri cautiously peeked out from their hiding place. As the dust settled, they saw Lari lying on the ground and raced over to him.

Denbo patted him none too gently on his face as Raeff spoke.

"Come on, Lari! Wake up!"

As Lari's eyes flickered open, Geri almost exploded with the kind of anger that's born from relief.

"You fool!" he shouted. " How could you do such a silly thing! In all honesty, I thought you had more sense!"

Denbo calmed him down.

"It's OK," he said quietly. "It was an accident. Be fair." Geri glared at him but settled down. Denbo continued. "Anyway, Lari's alright," and he turned to the elf on the ground who just at that moment moaned and tried to get up. "You are, aren't you?"

Lari nodded, then groaned again, and rubbed his head, where a large lump had appeared. Denbo broke off a bit of Aloe Vera that was growing nearby and squeezed out some of the gel.

"Here," he gave some to Lari. "Use that to rub on your lump, it might help."

"Thanks."

Lari rubbed his head then started to get up. With the help of the others, he finally struggled to his feet. When they let him go, he staggered around trying to get his balance, while the others tried hard not to laugh.

However, a loud burst of laughter did explode from the bush on their right.

Lari screwed up his face into a look of sheer disgust.

"Why do the kookaburras always laugh at the wrong moment?" he asked the rest of the group, who had started to laugh now, too.

"I think those kookas know *exactly* when to laugh," said Raeff in between his own laughter. "After all it is funny seeing you staggering around, and once they start, it's hard not to join in!"

Slowly but surely, the group got back to normal, although Lari was quiet and, from then on, much more careful.

They trudged on; aware that the trek to the only bird spider they knew about was quite a distance to travel. Nobody spoke much and their backpacks seemed to be getting heavier and heavier. They seemed to have been walking for ages.

Finally Raeff spoke.

"I don't know about any one else," he remarked to the whole group. "I'm hungry. Can we stop for a while, please?"

Denbo sighed.

"You're always hungry, Raeff. Don't you ever think of anything but food!"

Geri and Lari both looked at Denbo and said, at exactly the same time, "Can't see a problem with that!"

Raeff laughed and their spirits rose straight away. Denbo had to agree that it was definitely time they stopped for refreshments. They all looked for a cosy spot to spread out their picnic food and have a bit of a snooze.

***

Back at the village, Petula was still inconsolable. She didn't leave her home, and stayed in her room most of the time. Her wing remained useless and her shoulder felt like the troubles of the whole world were weighing it down. When she did come out of her room, she nagged at her mother all the time, asking how long the boys would be before they came back and her wing was fixed.

Her mother found it very difficult to be patient and understanding and hoped that the boys would be home soon so she could mend Petulas' wing and her daughter would once more be her cheery self.

CHAPTER 4

Mistaken identity

The boys were very happy to take off their backpacks and sit down for an early dinner in a little grove surrounded by colourful fungi. Lari and Geri were a bit upset, because they had already eaten the food they had packed, so Denbo and Raeff shared what they had. It wasn't long before they were contentedly chewing on the sandwiches they had brought with them.

Denbo sighed.

"Ahh!" he exhaled a long and drawn out breath of satisfaction. "Isn't this just the life," he said, turning to look at the other elves.

Raeff had started to drink a large gulp of his rosehip juice. Geri swallowed a rather large mouthful of dandelion salad sandwich and mumbled something no one understood.

There was silence again.

Before anyone could move, a rustling was heard in the

nearby bushes. Too at ease to react, the elves looked in the direction of the sound. The plants swayed, as if a mini earthquake was moving the earth.

Then a large echidna strolled into the clearing, knocking over a particularly nice group of mushrooms. He seemed distracted, and was astonished to see the four elves quietly lazing about on the small patch of lichen. His reaction was to stop moving and roll up quietly into a rather prickly ball.

No one moved.

No one spoke.

Gradually the echidna uncurled and blinked several times as he tried to focus on the group of elves. He was a little confused. What he saw in front of him were creatures that were bigger than any ants he had ever seen before. One of them moved. It was Raeff.

He crept forward and put out his hand.

"Hello," he said

The echidna immediately rolled up again.

Raeff looked at the other elves.

“I don’t think we have to worry too much about this fellow! If we can just get him to move on, we’ll be OK.”

He walked over and touched the large ball of quills.

“Ouch,” he said, jumping back rather quickly, “They are sharp!”

They all stood up and went over to Raeff. Geri put out his hand carefully and tried to feel the quills. They had never been so close to an echidna before. At that moment the echidna once again uncurled. Instead of the quills, Geri accidentally touched the snout, and a long thin tongue flicked out and wrapped around his hand.

“Whoa!” he shouted. “I’m not an ant!”

The echidna immediately began to curl up again, his tongue slipping quickly away. Lari grabbed at the disappearing snout.

“Don’t be so shy,” he said, gasping with the effort of holding on for dear life. “We will not hurt you!”

Geri was looking at his arm, and he screwed up his face in disgust.

“Yuk!” he exclaimed. “Talk about sticky! I think he took part of my skin away with his tongue.”

By this time, the echidna had stopped moving, and was looking at the elves with sorrowful eyes.

Raeff and Denbo were trying hard not to laugh. The echidna was huge when you were only 12cm tall, but seeing Geri and Lari dodging, weaving and jumping up and down around the animal was just too funny for words.

Suddenly a tear formed in the corner of one of the echidnas' eyes, then slowly trickled down to the ground. Instantly the elves were concerned.

" What's wrong?" Denbo asked anxiously.

"Please stop thinking of me as male," said a timid, quiet voice. "My name is Ava, and I'm lonely."

"Oh!" Denbo and the rest of the elves were most upset.

Raeff spoke for all of them when he said, "I'm so sorry. We just assumed..." and then there was silence.

She immediately rolled up again.

The elves looked at one another in dismay. What could they do? They all began to talk at once.

Geri put forward the idea that they should stop looking for the cobweb of the bird spider for Petulas' broken wing, and instead start searching for another echidna to be a friend for Ava. This suggestion caused such a hullabaloo that nobody notice Ava unroll and quietly creep away into the nearest clump of lomandra grass.

The elves quarrelled on, their voices getting ever higher until, suddenly, Denbo yelled.

"Enough!" he shouted, waving his arms furiously to get their attention. "Can't you see what you've done?"

The other three looked at him with confusion, shaking their heads at him as if he'd gone quite mad.

"What?" they all asked at once, wondering what he was talking about.

Denbo turned and gestured to the empty clearing.

Still the other elves looked at him blankly. Denbo said nothing. Once again he pointed to the empty space where Ava had been.

Suddenly, it dawned on Raeff, Geri and Lari. Lari looked bewildered.

"Where's Ava?" he asked, while Raeff and Geri looked at each other with amazement. Denbo shook his head with frustration and shrugged his shoulders, almost angrily.

"Well, as you can see, she's gone. You were so busy

‘discussing’ her predicament that you forgot all about her!”

“We’ll have to find her and apologise.” Geri said sorrowfully. ‘I wonder how far away she’s gone?”

They looked around the area with some confusion, wondering if they could pick up any signs to indicate where Ava had gone. There were several scuffle marks on the ground, but Lari and Denbo got into a fight about the interpretations. It began to look like there would be actual physical violence, so Geri stepped in and told them to stop.

“This isn’t achieving anything,” he said. “By now Ava will either be ages away or curled up in a little ball hiding - she will be so afraid with all your shouting!”

Finally they decided on a plan of action. Raeff surprised them all with his calm logic.

“If we spread out in all directions - each one taking a quarter of a circle, and search for a couple of hours - we should be able to at least find something, and still not get lost! We’ll meet back here when the sun is nearly set, before it gets too dark.”

They all agreed and began their search, fanning out in all

directions.

About ten minutes later Lari was heard to shout.

"I've found her!"

They all turned and made their way to his voice, excited that Ava was so close.

When they arrived they were surprised to see Lari baled up by an angry echidna that was well and truly bristling with agitation. The snout was poking Lari in the stomach and Lari could go no further. He was backed up against a small sapling, which was trembling as much as Lari! The other elves looked at the situation with amazement, and Denbo raced forward

"Ava!" he yelled as he ran. "What's got into you?"

The echidna was momentarily distracted and turned towards Denbo. Lari, who relaxed visibly, shook his head and suddenly felt the need to gasp some much-needed air.

"It's not..."

Denbo by this time had come to a skidding halt and so had

the echidna. They faced each other and glared. It was the quiet voice of Raeff from behind Denbo that soothed the situation.

"I'm sorry, sir!" he whispered. "We mistook you for a friend of ours."

Everything went quiet. The echidna seemed to blink uncertainly. At this moment Geri came out from under a nearby orchid and began to laugh.

Everyone turned to him with amazement and Raeff put his fingers to his lips to quieten him.

Geri was almost doubled over with hilarity.

"I don't believe it!" he spluttered. "Twice in one day! Fancy that!"

The echidna looked astonished and grunted.

"What are you talking about?" he said.

It took a little time, but eventually Herb (because that was the echidnas' name) saw the funny side of the situation. He was most impressed that Ava was somewhere close, and declared that he was off to search for her himself. He scurried off into the bush leaving the elves looking at one another with something like relief.

"Well," said Denbo. "With every bit of luck, that will solve everyone's problem. Ava won't be lonely, Herb won't be angry, and we don't have to go in search of Ava to apologise - I'm sure Herb will explain!"

Everyone nodded in agreement. They sat down for a late afternoon raspberry tea and, while Denbo divided up a ripe fig that had fallen from a nearby tree, they began to discuss their next move.

CHAPTER 5

The journey continues.

After all the excitement with Ava and Herb, late afternoon tea was a welcome interlude. The noises of the two echidnas had faded into the distance and the boys all lazed about the clearing. Several minutes past in slumberous silence and the only sound was the chirping of crickets in the distance. Every now and then the chattering of a small family of birds gave the air an almost out-of-this world feel.

Denbo broke the peacefulness with a low murmur.

"We always seem to be stopping, eating and snoozing! This has got to stop!" he looked around at the group, still lazing around as if they had not a care in the world.

"I s'pose we'd better move on, otherwise we'll never get the webbing for Petula!" he commented to no one in particular. "There's still a good two hours of light left before we need to organise the camp for the night!"

Nobody moved.

Denbo tried again.

"Come on! Move!" he said crossly.

The elves blinked and began to straighten up and gather themselves together to continue their expedition. Everyone felt lazy and didn't really feel like resuming their journey, but after a little while, as they began to move through the forest, their natural joy came back.

They walked on, chatting and laughing. No problems stopped the happy little band. The afternoon passed, and the sun began to slowly sink below the trees to the west. The sky turned a burnt orange and the few clouds turned into purple streaks. The shadows grew longer and the night breeze began to stir the leaves of the trees above them. Eventually they realised it was time to stop and set up a camp.

Denbo and Raeff set Lari and Geri the task of collecting some soft moss to make up some beds. Denbo wove together some large leaves of a fern to give them some shelter, and Raeff organised a feast of mushrooms and a yummy dessert of berries for their meal.

It wasn't long, before the four friends had settled for the night, their stomachs full and their beds comfy. The camp went quiet and the elves slept.

***

Young Jac was still smouldering with a quiet anger that Denbo and Raeff had not asked him to go with them. All his life he had battled with teasing and the rest of the elves avoiding him. He'd had enough!

He felt friendless.

Then, when Geri and Lari actually sneaked away without him, it was the last straw. He thought about it all the time, and finally decided on his plan of attack.

That night, while the elves slept in the forest, and the fairies in the village were tucked up and asleep in their beds, he crept out of the village. His self-righteous anger smothered his fear of the dark and the unknown. He took with him a pack of food and a struggling glow-worm on a lead, to help him see in the dark.

"Stop it!" he hissed at the worm as it wriggled and pulled on the lead. His face was contorted with his rage, and he yanked the glow-worm with all his might, onto the path.

“I don’t want to go!” cried Rhonda, the glow-worm, and her light flickered and almost went out.

“If you don’t behave,” Jac growled at the poor little glow-worm. “I will tell your family you were the one that lit the way for Ruby, the red-back spider, to discover the Queen’s favourite pet wasp’s stash of insects that he then ate!”

Rhonda decided it was probably best to go along with Jac’s ideas, at least until Jac calmed down and realised that he was being just a mite silly!

Jac continued into the night, pulling Rhonda along constantly. He didn’t seem to get tired and mumbled under his breath all the time. Rhonda couldn’t make much sense of what he said, but occasionally she heard a ‘Denbo’ or ‘Lari’ mentioned.

Jac wasn’t slowing down and he certainly wasn’t calming down!

They moved through the bush at an amazing pace until Jac could go no further. He sat down on a small emerging toadstool and told Rhonda to go home. The glow-worm couldn’t get away fast enough!

For some time Jac sat in the darkness, wondering why he had set out on this venture. He was just a little bit frightened, and was annoyed with himself that he had let Rhonda go home.

The annoyance ate into his being, and turned once more into hate and rage.

"If Lari and Geri had taken me with them," he thought to himself. " I wouldn't feel like this!" The thoughts ran around in circles in his mind until the fear disappeared and he jumped up and began to go towards the direction of the bird spider's web.

***

Denbo and the other elves slept on. The night was cool and comfortable and even the mosquitoes were lazy. A cricket or two chirped to each other and several night birds moved around the bush on silent wings. A native mouse or two came upon the camp, but after a careful sniff at the quiet bodies, they moved on. Every now and again Raeff snored, and Lari fidgeted on his soft bed of lichen.

***

Jac suddenly began to be aware that there were sounds in the bush. He stood still and listened. He heard the soft monotonous boom of a Tawny Frogmouth somewhere to his north. A rustling in the grass near a large Eucalypt on his left gave him the shivers, but it turned out to be a small night gecko, darting around disturbing insects in the dark. A series of loud chirps told him that several crickets were nearby.

A disturbing buzzing heralded the approach of a mosquito and Jac clambered quickly behind a fern and hid in its shadow. The mosquito moved on, and then, just as Jac was about to travel on, he heard a noise that made him stand very still and take notice.

He could have sworn it was someone snoring!

He crept towards the sound.

A clump of grass blocked his view, and he reached out to part the strappy leaves trying to peer through them in the darkness.

Just at that moment the moon came out from behind a cloud and Jac was able to see the camp. Raeff turned over onto his side and stopped snoring, and at the same moment Geri stretched out an arm in his sleep and hit a small rock. He yelped and awoke with a start.

All the elves awoke and grumbled at him.

Jac jumped back into hiding, hoping he wouldn't be seen.

The clouds slid across the sky and obscured the moon again, and everyone settled down once more. Jac decided to get some sleep himself and curled up under the grass and began to snooze.

***

When the sun rose the following morning, a light mist

covered the area. The four elves awoke and shook away the moisture and the sleep from their bodies.

Raeff peered into the trees, and stretched.

"I hate mornings!" he grumbled.

Denbo laughed, and Lari and Geri turned to see what was funny. Raeff looked at them all with sleepy eyes as he scratched his head and ruffled his hair so that it was sticking up in all directions.

In the cover of the grass, Jac awoke and peered through the stalks at him too. He shivered a little in the cool morning air, as a tiny breeze rustled the leaves of the grass slightly.

He ducked back quickly when Raeff seemed to look right at him. Now was not the time to be discovered! He was going to make those elves sorry they wouldn't let him join them!

***

Slowly but surely the elves began to get ready for their next day's journey. Raeff jammed his hat on his head, and his hair poked out the side. No one even noticed. They all looked a bit bedraggled after the sleep-out in the bush. Lari had put his jumper on backwards and was trying to fix the problem. Geri sat tiredly looking at his mug, hoping it would fill magically with hot tea.

Denbo was the only one who seemed to be alert. He began to look at a rough map he had folded up and put in his backpack before he had left home.

“We’ll have to hurry today,” he remarked to the group. “The bird spider’s web was about a day’s walk away from here the last time it was seen. We should get there just before dark if everything goes OK.”

Lari and Geri were still waking up, and Denbo knew they had not heard him.

He raised his voice a little, and Jac ducked back in alarm thinking he may have been seen. The next words, though, made him grin to himself.

“Come on, you two.” Denbo was saying crossly to the sleepy elves. “We didn’t bring you along to slow us down. That’s why we didn’t ask you - after all, you were the ones who found us. Now! Get a move on!”

So - Lari and Geri weren’t welcome either!

***

Eventually the little band of elves got under way and, as the sun began to twinkle through the leaves of the canopy overhead, they began to enjoy the walk. The forest floor was damp, and every now and again, a small lizard or insect rustled the undergrowth. They chatted, laughed and occasionally burst into song.

Not far behind them, Jac followed quietly, carefully observing the bush surrounding him as he walked.

Suddenly, in the trees in front of the noisy elves, Jac saw a hive of honeybees. They were not native bees, and there were a lot of them. He began to quicken his pace, and keeping a watchful eye on the progress of Denbo and the friends, he scurried around the group, hiding in the bushes and arriving before them, near the bees.

He picked up a long stick, and when he stood under the hive, he gave an almighty swing with it, in order to hit the hive and annoy the bees.

Instead, his foot caught in a small hole and he tripped, falling heavily on the damp and smelly leaves.

He felt dazed and he sat up slowly and checked to see if anything was hurt. Cautiously he stood up, and looked about for the stick.

Raeff's voice was suddenly very loud and very off key!

"What a beautiful day today!" he sang, and the other elves all laughed and began to pelt him with crumpled up leaves.

"Heavens!" Lari screwed up his face in mock dismay as he looked at Raeff, clamping his hands over his ears at the same time. "What have we ever done to you! Wow! What a terrible voice!"

Jac realised that if he didn't move and hide immediately, he would be discovered. He looked around quickly and saw a great spot to hide. He ran under the tuft of grass and ran smack bang into a small sapling of a stinging tree.

It was all he could do to stop crying out in pain, as the tiny new leaves grazed his arm and started the painful sting. He cowered down out of sight, looking desperately around for some aloe so he could rub some of the gel on his arm to ease the sting.

About three metres away on the other side of the track, he could see a plant, but he had to wait for the four elves to go laughing past before he could risk going over to it to help ease his pain.

The group of elves passed by, under the hive, and the moment past when he could have sabotaged their task.

He trudged over the pathway, grabbed a small bit of aloe, squeezed out some of the gel, and thankfully rubbed it into his stinging arm. The pain faded away, and Jac immediately began to plan his next attempt at frustrating the groups' plans. He thought and thought, but nothing came to mind. He decided to keep following, and if a great opportunity came his way, he would take advantage as soon as he could.

CHAPTER 6.

The bird spider found.

Afterwards, they all agreed the day had gone quicker than they thought it had. They had been walking for what seemed hours and had stopped every now and again for a rest and something to eat. The afternoon had seen them walking along at a similar speed to the morning. They had laughed and joked, and nothing had gone wrong. The afternoon was nearly over and the sun had begun to disappear behind a hill to the west - it wouldn't be long before it would be setting. Finally, the elves came around a corner when Denbo unexpectedly stopped and just stared. Raeff bumped into him and then the whole group looked up and stood still, astonished.

There above them, strung from a sapling to a large fig tree and anchored to the ground nearby, hung a magnificent spider's web.

It was huge and strong, and very high.

Caught in its intricate pattern were several large insects, including a praying mantis and a large beetle. A couple of dragonflies fluttered wearily, exhausted, in their last bid for freedom. Over in the left-hand corner, hidden slightly by the leaves of the sapling, the spider busily wrapped a poor unfortunate cockroach that had flown into the web during the night. This spider would not be going hungry!

Denbo swallowed nervously. The others turned and looked at him with wide eyes as they heard the gulp.

"Gosh!" said Raeff in a stifled whisper. "That spider's as big as us!"

"I think it might be even bigger!" Denbo commented.

Lari and Geri didn't move. They seemed glued to the spot.

Jac, still out of sight, crawled through the undergrowth and moved around until he was on the other side of the web to the others. He, too, looked at the spider and its web with awe and fear. Slowly an idea formed in his mind.

Denbo was the first one to move

"Well, there's no use just looking at it," he said with a shake of his head. "We came to do a job. Let's try and work out a plan."

He moved towards a group of tiny mushrooms that were just beginning to break the surface of the soil underneath the large tree that the spider's web was attached to.

Lari blinked and flexed his shoulders and began to follow.

"Oh! Yuk!" he exclaimed and came to another stop, his nose wrinkled with disgust.

"What?" asked Geri as Raeff looked at him and raised his eyebrows.

"Look!" Lari shuddered.

Everyone turned their gaze in the direction of Lari's pointed finger.

Under the web was a small hillock. When Raeff moved towards it to have a closer look, he too, looked horrified and leapt back towards Geri.

"Yuk!" he said. "That's a heap of empty insect skeletons!" he said with a look of revulsion.

The group of elves stood and looked at the pile with an

awful fascination. Once again they couldn't seem to move.

Jac, hidden behind a clump of grass, was also horrified. It really was a most dangerous spider, and Jac almost decided to forget his plans. It just didn't seem worthwhile having one of his 'friends' hurt too much. Who knows what could happen? He glanced up towards the spider. It had finished wrapping up the cockroach, and was obviously ready to move towards the centre of its web once more.

Jac hurriedly looked around him, as the four others began to talk amongst themselves. He heard Lari say, in rather a whiny voice.

"Really, Denbo, can't we forget this!"

Jac peeked through the grass. He saw Denbo put his hands on his hips and glare at Lari. Then he spoke rather crossly.

"Listen, Lari, I came to do a job for my sister. I didn't ask you to come along - you just did! Now we have to work out what we are going to do!" the group began to walk away, arguing quite loudly, and, as their voices began to fade, Jac found what he had been looking for.

He saw a small pebble that he could lift and threw it with all his strength. It went flying through the air and hit the spider's web. As the vibrations from the small stone moved through the web the spider scuttled quickly towards the disturbance.

Jac heard a cry of dismay from one of the elves, he wasn't sure which one, and then there was a moment of deathly quiet.

When he peered through the grass again, he saw Geri dangling from the web; caught by the thread the spider had anchored on the ground. He had been stepping carefully over it when the stone had hit. The vibrations had caused the thread to wobble and it had snagged his foot. He had fallen, flinging his hands out in front of himself, causing the web to tangle even more. Now the spider was pulling the web's thread tight, and Geri had left the ground, turned upside down, and was wriggling about and calling out to the others for help.

Raeff yelled.

"Stop moving! You are attracting the spider!"

Jac was not pleased. This hadn't really been his plan - he had only wanted the spider to move suddenly and give the elves a real scare. Once again everything had gone wrong. Things were getting out of hand.

The spider was getting closer and closer to Geri and Jac closed his eyes. Denbo had started to scramble up the tree to try and reach the terrified elf. Raeff was waving his arms about trying to distract the spider. Lari was sitting on a small mushroom looking stunned and afraid.

Jac began to move from his hiding place. Perhaps, he thought, he should help. Explain that he hadn't meant this to happen.

Suddenly, out of the trees, a large bird flew down. It plucked Geri from the web.

The spider's web was broken.

Geri screamed.

Chaos followed.

Denbo leapt from the tree trunk and grabbed at the free-floating strand of webbing. It stuck to his hand in the process and he swung through the air, spread-eagling himself on the main section of the web. Raeff tumbled over and landed near an ant's nest and yelped as several ants swarmed towards him. Lari fell off the mushroom and began to howl. Jac stood still, petrified, his eyes as big as saucers, as the spider began to move towards Denbo.

What were they going to do?

Before any one could do anything, the large bird that had grabbed Geri flew back and seized Denbo by his leg, pulling him away from the web, just as the spider was about to pounce.

Raeff had forgotten the ants and ducked as the bird flew towards him. He became aware that the bird was taking Denbo to an area just out of sight. He ran over to the spot and saw the bird gently lower Denbo to the ground next to the crumpled body of Geri.

"Hey!" he yelled.

The bird turned and then Raeff realised there was no danger. He smiled.

"Wow!" he said and came over and almost hugged the bird. "Thank you so much, Wally!"

By this time Denbo was sitting up trying to brush some of the sticky web off of his clothes. A small pile of the web was at his feet. He, too, spoke to Wally.

"How an earth did you know where we were?" he asked gruffly.

Wally preened his feathers and cooed quietly.

"I've been watching you," he said. "When your mother told me about the strange 'bird' spider, I was concerned and followed you."

At that point Geri groaned, and tried to sit up. He looked dreadful - his face was pale from the shock, his clothes were dirty and there was a long length of web dangling from the leg that had been entangled. He yanked it off his leg and crumpled it into a ball and threw it on the ground. He was very pleased to get rid of it.

Both Denbo and Raeff went to him and began to help him to his feet.

"Where's Lari?" Denbo looked at Raeff and raised one eyebrow.

"Here I am!" came a voice.

When he came into sight, he was leading a cowering and unhappy Jac.

Wally cleared his throat and remarked.

“Oh! I was going to tell you about him. From up in the canopy, he wasn’t hard to spot!” And with that, he took off before any one could thank him and disappeared into the trees.

Lari led Jac forward and, holding on to his jacket with a tight grip, pushed him in front of Denbo. Jac glared at Lari then saw Denbo looking at him. He sniffed back a sob.

“I’m sorry,” he said. “I didn’t mean...” He squirmed and grimaced, pulling at his jacket.

Lari let go. Instead of running away, Jac sat down with a thud, then looked up at Denbo. Denbo was surprised to see tears in Jac’s eyes.

“I didn’t want anyone hurt.” Jac said while he rocked backwards and forwards slightly. “But you didn’t even ask me to come. You snuck away from me as if I was useless. I thought you were my friends!”

Denbo swallowed his anger. The words he had been going to say died in his throat. He looked at Jac, sitting there looking all dejected, and he just couldn’t yell at him.

“You’re right,” he said as the others looked on with amazement. Then he patted Jac on his shoulder. Jac groaned. Denbo looked at his friends who were standing still with their mouths open.

“What are you lot looking at,” he said gruffly. “Come on, lets get ourselves organised and set up camp before we head off home.”

Denbo looked at the pile of webbing that was at his feet.

“Well,” he added. “At least we got the web for Mum to fix Petula’s wing.”

CHAPTER 7

On the way home.

Raeff looked around and checked to find out where the spider was hiding. Then he snorted.

“Well, I don’t know about you,” Raeff said. “I’m not setting up camp for the night so close to that spider. We’ve got to get out of here first, and then, in the morning, we’ve got to get home!”

Geri and Lari looked as if they had both been hit by a cyclone; they looked completely stunned. Jac was still sitting quietly groaning, looking down at the earth between his feet. Denbo looked at Raeff, then Geri and Lari in turn. His lips compressed and he shook his head as if he was annoyed. He shrugged, then turned to Jac.

“No use looking at the ground,” he commented wryly. “It won’t open up and swallow you.”

There was silence for a moment, then the web above the ground shimmered and the spider moved to fix his web. The elves stood transfixed, looking at the spider. Denbo, still looking at the spider, bent and picked up the ball of web on the ground.

"Come on!" he said and the group turned and began to move towards the track that would take them home. Jac got up and stumbled after the group. There were several nervous looks back to the spider that was now busy cocooning a wriggling grasshopper and had fortunately lost interest in the little band.

No word was uttered for about ten minutes, then Raeff let out a long breath, as if he had been holding it for the whole time.

"Stop!" he said, holding up his hand and putting his other on his chest. He sounded out of breath and sat down abruptly in the leaves on the track. Raeff looked pale.

The forest had now begun to get dark as the sun slid away for the night. The trees were thick and no one could see any stars either.

"What's wrong?" Denbo asked, his face showing concern as he looked at his friend.

Raeff sighed.

"I think all that excitement and worry has just caught up with me," he said. "I feel exhausted."

"I understand," Denbo replied. "I think we all feel a bit like that. Let's find a nice spot right now and set up our camp for the night."

It was only a few moments later that they were all looking at a little clearing, with a large puddle in the middle. A mother green tree frog was sitting quietly on a rock next to the water. She hardly moved, but the elves could see that she was guarding a froth of eggs that she must have laid in the puddle.

Denbo turned to the boys.

“Let’s stop here,” he said. “It seems like a safe place. I’m sure Mother Frog wouldn’t be here if it wasn’t!”

The frog croaked suddenly, and everyone jumped. Geri and Lari were still holding Jac, and they all fell over together in a heap in their surprise.

“I will stay here,” Mother Frog said in a very gruff voice, as if she had a cold. “You all look as if you need some sleep - I will keep watch for you.”

Denbo walked over and patted her on her shoulder.

“Thank you,” he said. “We are all exhausted. We have had a terrible experience today.”

All the elves began talking at once, except Jac who just looked on with wide teary eyes. They were trying to tell her what had happened.

Mother Frog nodded and sat still. She didn't seem to be impressed.

"Yes, I know that spider," she croaked. "He is not very nice - and Mr. Nobblyback, our local Cane Toad Elder, says he isn't even edible!"

***

The next morning, all the elves felt much better. They had had a lovely sleep without having to worry about any dangers. Raeff awoke first, and woke the others.

"Mother Frog has gone!" he told them. "I wonder when she left?"

Denbo walked over to the puddle. Mother Frog's eggs were still safe, and he could see tiny black wriggling dots of tadpoles in some of them.

“Well, everything looks OK,” he murmured and then had to hold back Geri and Lari because they nearly fell in the water as they scrambled to look at the eggs as well.

The next thing they had to do was have breakfast. While they were eating, Lari and Geri told Denbo and Raeff what Jac had done before he was caught. Jac had been so upset last night that he had told them everything. Now Jac sat quietly and didn’t say a word.

After their breakfast of bread and honey, it was time to start their trip back home.

“Come on, everyone,” Denbo said as he gathered up the ball of web. He put it into a sack he had carried in his backpack and handed the sack to Jac.

“Here,” he told the subdued and still unhappy elf. “Considering what you’ve been doing to try and stop us in this journey, I think you should carry this back to the village.”

Jac glared at him but took the sack and began to trudge off down a small pathway between two ferns.

As the morning wore on and the sun warmed the air the elves began to laugh and sing. Slowly but surely Jac lost his frown and joined in. Everyone was friends again, and the elves were enjoying the trip. Soon they would be home, and Petula's wing would be fixed and everything would get back to normal again.

Without any warning, a loud bang made them all stop.

"What was that?" Lari whispered.

In the distance a lot of noise was disturbing the bush. The elves looked at one another in confusion. Denbo was the first to move.

"I think we'd better hide," he said. "And it would be a good idea to find a very safe hiding spot!"

Everyone immediately began to look for a safe hiding spot. The noise seemed to be getting closer and louder. The undergrowth in the distance began to rustle and shake.

Raeff called and waved his hand frantically. "Over here! Hurry!"

Geri and Lari raced over to him. Denbo grabbed Jac and then followed. Raeff had found a small hole underneath the huge buttress root of a strangler fig tree. They all crawled into it and then peered cautiously out to see if they could find out what was making such a ruckus among the trees.

Suddenly a large foot came down to the ground not far from them. They all ducked back out of sight quickly.

"I don't believe it!" exclaimed Jac. "It's a human!"

"I know," replied Raeff and Denbo together. Geri and Lari were both amazed.

“I’ve never seen one like that before!” muttered Lari. “The only other human I’ve seen is Granny Flannigan, and she can’t see very well.”

“And even if she could, I think she would be kind. This one is a man - and he has a gun.” Denbo silenced them all with a finger to his lips. “That was the bang we heard before!”

“Why is he shooting?” asked Geri.

“I don’t know,” answered Denbo in a whisper.

Raeff looked as if he was about to race out of their hiding place.

“What is he shooting at! That’s what I’d like to know!” Raeff was ready for a fight.

“I’ll go and stamp on his foot!” he said, but Denbo held him back.

“Don’t be so foolish,” Denbo cautioned. “There might be a dangerous animal around, too. Maybe that’s what he’s shooting at!”

Then they heard the human say sssh to some one that was out of sight.

“Hey, mate,” the human near them whispered. “The wallaby’s up there. Keep it quiet.”

Raeff was now hopping around ready to do anything to save the wallaby.

"Stop!" Denbo insisted, holding him by his jacket and getting Geri and Lari to hold Jac as well.

"Firstly, that is impossible. The human is much too large for you to do anything to. Secondly he could stand on you without even knowing, and thirdly - the wallaby can hear them. If they think they are being quiet, then they are very much mistaken!"

"But what can we do?" asked Raeff.

"Nothing!" Denbo shook his head. "We will just have to wait it out down here until they move on."

The elves all sat down gloomily in their hiding place and waited. It seemed like forever, but it had only been a few minutes when Geri mentioned that he couldn't hear any noise outside.

Just as he spoke, another very loud bang was heard and then the sound of running feet echoed through the forest. The whole ground seemed to vibrate.

The elves clambered to their feet and Lari reached the entrance to their hole first.

"I think they have gone," he declared turning to the rest of his group. "Gosh, I hope the wallaby escaped!"

They all emerged from their hidey-hole and peered around. There didn't seem to be anyone around, and there was silence again.

Suddenly they dashed back towards their safe hole as a bird came fluttering down almost on top of them.

Jac stood up, walked out of the hole and glared at the bird.

"What do you want?" he asked rudely.

"Hang on, Jac," Raeff said. "This is Wally - don't you remember. He was the one who saved us all back at the bird spider! Just because he dobbed you in doesn't mean you have to be rude!"

Denbo came and stood before Wally.

“Is there anything wrong?” he asked.

Wally cooed and bobbed his head in obvious distress.

“Yes!” he said. “I wasn’t quite quick enough to warn the wallaby about the hunters. He got shot in the leg and he needs your help. At the moment he’s managed to escape the humans, but he is in a lot of pain.”

“Right’” said Denbo, taking charge immediately. “Geri, go and find some Aloe Vera for his wound. Raeff, I’ll need some more spider’s web to wrap the wound. Take Lari with you and pick up some of the bird spider’s web that we left on the ground from Geris' encounter back at her lair. I’ll take Jac and find the wallaby.”

As everyone rushed to do the jobs Denbo looked at Wally. “What’s the wallaby’s name?” he asked.

“It’s Warren,” Wally answered. “But you should hurry, he’s in a lot of pain and losing quite a lot of blood!”

“OK,” Denbo said turning to Jac. “Here, Jac. Look after all these bundles.” He gathered all of the backpacks that had been left on the ground when the other elves had rushed off and heaved Lari’s' and Geri’s toward Jac. Then he shouldered Raeff’s bag with his own and Jac picked up the others.

“Lead on, Wally!” he said. “Come on, Jac. Let’s move out!”

CHAPTER 8.

A little detour.

Wally flew low from branch to branch so that Denbo who had Raeff's backpack, and Jac, who carried the luggage of both Geri and Lari, could keep up.

Eventually they reached a thicket of vines, twisted around a large tree. Wally hopped down onto the ground and pushed through the tangle beckoning to Denbo and Jac with his wing.

The two elves crawled through the mass of leaves and vine, noticing a trail of blood. Inside they found a small refuge carved out in the centre. In front of them lay a very unhappy wallaby, with tears on his cheeks and blood on his tail. One of his back legs was crooked and had a hole in it from which the blood was flowing.

Denbo made comforting noises as he moved forwards. Jac shuffled around, obviously a little nervous around such a big animal. Wally flew to a spot near Warren's head and cooed softly.

After the wallaby had accepted them, and Denbo was ready to look at the wound on his leg, he asked Wally to take his handkerchief to some water and soak it and bring it back. While Wally was doing that, Denbo had a closer look at the wound.

“Thank goodness,” he remarked to himself. Then he spoke to Wally in a comforting voice.“ The bullet went right through, and luckily didn’t do any serious damage. I know it hurts, but there are no vital arteries or organs in that area.”

The wallaby tried to look brave.

“There now,” Denbo added. “It won’t take long. I’ll have it all cleaned up and on its way to being healed in no time at all.”

At that moment Wally came back with the handkerchief and water in a little container made from a hollowed out piece of wood. At the same time, Geri arrived with some Aloe, and with Jacs’ help began to extract some gel from inside the leaves.

Denbo was most pleased. “Thank you,” he nodded to Wally. “Perhaps you could go and lead the others to this spot, if you wouldn’t mind.”

As Wally flew off again, Denbo turned to Jac. “You’ll have to help me here,” he said. “I’ll need someone to keep Warren still while I clean the wound and pack it with the aloe gel.” Jac looked a little scared and pale, but nodded his head firmly. He felt that at last he was accepted by the group, and doing his part to help.

It took Denbo a little more time that he had anticipated to fix Warren’s leg. Just as he was winding web from his ball of web around the leg, Lari, Raeff and Wally appeared cautiously at the entrance of the refuge.

Raeff spoke at once. He seemed upset.

“Why did you make me go back to the bird spider’s web? The spider looked bigger than ever, and glared at me with its beady eyes! I thought I was going to be eaten! Lucky we’d left that bit of web from Geris' leg on the ground.” He stopped just long enough to take another breath, and before Denbo could say anything, he continued. “And after all that, I get here and find you using the web you already had! It’s not fair!”

“Settle, Raeff!” Denbo grinned at his friend. “I knew we’d have to have that extra web, otherwise we would not have enough for Mum to fix Petula’s wing.”

“Oh!” Raeff shrugged, and immediately calmed down. “Can I do anything to help?”

“It’s fine,” answered Denbo. “I’m nearly finished here.”

While Denbo finished off winding the web around Warren's wound, Geri, Lari, Raeff, Wally and Jac sat and watched quietly. Soon Warren looked a little better and Denbo suggested that he rest and allow nature to help fix his leg.

"Before we leave," he said to his little band of elves. "We should make sure Warren has enough water and grass nearby to last him for a few hours until he has a little more strength and can get about a bit."

Geri got up straight away to go and find some grass.

"I'm glad we could help you Warren," Lari said as he followed Geri out of the little sanctuary.

"And that the human didn't find you!" added Jac.

Raeff looked at Denbo and a silent thought crossed between them - it could have been a lot worse!

When Warren's needs had been met, and Denbo was assured that everything would be fine, the band got together and said goodbye.

As the little group of adventurers organized themselves to get back home, Wally flew up into the canopy of the forest.

"I'll keep a watch on Warren," he assured them all. "When I can, I'll report back to your village. Safe trip home." then he flew back to overlook Warren's health and wellbeing.

"Thank you," the elves called and then they were on their way once more.

CHAPTER 9

Are we there yet?

It was a subdued team of elves that shouldered their backpacks and left Warren and Wally and started back towards home. No one spoke for almost half an hour as they trudged along an overgrown track that hadn't been used for a long time.

Geri finally broke the silence.

"Gosh, if I'd have known this was going to be so tiring I wouldn't have been so anxious to come!"

"Yeah, me too!" agreed Lari.

Raeff snorted. "Well, that's why we didn't ask you!" and he turned towards Jac. "Or you!"

Denbo sighed as he saw Geris' face sadden and Lari pat his friend on the shoulder. Jac began to scowl, and Denbo knew there would be a fight if he wasn't quick and careful.

“Stop it Raeff,” he said. “I don’t think I would have come along if I’d have known it was going to be this hard either!” Geri gave Denbo a look of gratitude, and Raeff mumbled to himself, but didn’t say any more.

Denbo continued, “And, do you realize that it’s already lunch time and with all the excitement, we haven’t even thought of food, especially you, Raeff!” and he grinned at Raeff, and Raeff grinned back weakly.

“Well,” Raeff said, already looking and sounding a little more cheerful. “What are we waiting for?” With that, he promptly sat down in the middle of the path, under a tussock of grass and looked at them all.

“What are we going to have? Any one for roast cockroach with beetle salad?”

They all groaned. That wasn’t their idea of a good feed.

“I saw a few figs on the ground just a bit back. Do you want me to get them?" Geri looked around eagerly. He really wanted to feel as if he was useful now. Raeff's comment had hurt his pride.

"Yes, please," they all said at once. Geri smiled and dashed off back in the direction they had just come.

It wasn't long before they heard Geri calling for help, with shouts of 'give me that' in between.

Raeff sighed and got to his feet, By that time, all the others had raced off to help Geri.

When they burst into the area where Geri was, they saw him struggling to hold on to a fig, pulling with all his might. At the other end, also pulling, was a young mouse. As soon as it saw the group of elves, it let go of the fig and ran off. Geri tumbled onto his back

Everyone, including Geri, burst into laughter. Finally good cheer was once again restored, and they all sat down and enjoyed the figs. About fifteen minutes later, Raeff stood up and patted his rather round stomach.

“Oh! But that was good.” he said. “I’m full!”

Denbo laughed.

“We’d better get on our way - while we can.” There was silence as everyone looked, puzzled, at Denbo, but then he added. “It won’t be long before Raeff’s hungry again - I’d like to be home by then!” And they all understood.

Once more they began on their way along the track, and finally turned into a more familiar path. They knew they were nearly home.

CHAPTER 10

Everyone is happy.

When the boys finally reached the hill before home, Jac stopped and asked everyone to forgive him for his foolish feelings and actions earlier.

"Of course," Denbo said and turned to the others and raised his eyebrows in query. They all nodded in agreement. Nobody could stay angry long - it just wasn't the way they were.

"Anyway, I'm too tired to hold grudges," remarked Raeff. "We really don't mind. I think I would have been cranky, too."

They all trudged wearily up that last hill, and when they reached the top they were surprised. Coming up the hill towards them were several of the Queens' soldiers. They were carrying a flag and were all in their best dress uniforms. A band of merry musicians behind them started to play a rousing march.

On the edge of their tiny village a crowd of the villagers began to cheer and wave their own colourful flags. Wally stood nearby looking proud, and next to him stood Petula's mother. Holding her hand was Petula, her broken wing still hanging uselessly from her shoulder, but now she was smiling.

Denbo and Raeff were amazed by the reception. Lari, Geri and especially Jac were definitely over-awed by it all.

Queen Isabella presided over the wonderful welcoming banquet, and afterwards Denbo was shocked to receive a very special award for bravery. Everyone kept exclaiming over the boys.

"Fancy being so close to a bird spider," Jacs' younger brother Chryso said. It made Jac hang his head in shame, but no one noticed. They were all astounded that the group had survived.

"You don't know the half of it," declared Raeff, and proceeded to tell everyone the awful moments at the web, and how Wally had actually been their saviour. He made sure he didn't tell them about any of Jacs' actions. After all they had forgiven him and he didn't want Jac to feel that he was to blame.

When Queen Isabella heard the story, she called Wally over, and hung a gold medallion around his neck. Wally was too choked up with emotion to even utter a single 'coo', but he strutted around the village later, with his chest puffed out. He was very proud of his medal and showed it to any one who cared to look.

The party lasted well into the night. Gradually everyone began to drift away, and by the time the glowworms were starting to fade, they had disappeared into their homes, exhausted but happy.

The next morning Petula's mother was up early, singing a catchy tune as she did her chores.

Petula came downstairs, wiping the sleep from her eyes, her wing looking particularly bedraggled.

"Come on, dear," her mother cheerfully bustled around her. "Now we've got the web, I can get started - before you know where you are, you'll be back to normal." Petula smiled, but didn't move. Her mother continued, this time mumbling to herself. "Where an earth did I put the tape measure?"

This time Petula giggled, and she put her hand into her mothers' apron pocket and pulled out the tape.

"There you are," she said, then she twirled around so her mother could measure the tear in her wing.

In a twinkling of an eye, Petula's mother had woven her magic around the spiders' web and a shimmering piece of wing was ready to be stitched into place. With tender fingers and careful movements, Petula's mother had fixed her daughters' wing without Petula feeling a thing.

"Thank you so much, Mum," she said and hugged her mother so tightly that she let out a squeak and asked her daughter to let her go.

"It wasn't only me, you know, she said with a smile. "Without Denbo and the boys help, this wouldn't have been possible!"

"I know, Mum," Petula replied. "I'm off to see Daisy and Pansy. While I am on my way, I'll make a special trip to thank them, as well as Wally, too."

Her mother waved as she lifted effortlessly into the sky. Petula twirled around in delight, once more free and able to fly, and then she was off to her next adventure.

Book two of the series will be available in 2014, with book 3 coming fairly soon thereafter.

For other books by this author, please go to her webpage. Ebooksbymaureenlarter.com.

You will find picture books for children:
Angus Ant and the Acrobats
Betty Bee's Birthday Bash
Ben Brolga's Band
Gardening guides
Summer
Autumn
Winter
Spring
All books are available in ebooks (PDF files) as well as hard copies. There are more illustrations in the hard copies and PDF range.
There is also a range of merchandise available.
('Broken Wing' will be available as an ebook in June 2013)

Please enjoy the following excerpt from book two

The Elves of Aurora

CHAPTER ONE

Raeff gets angry.

"Denbo!" called Mistress Gondola as she saw Denbo strolling along the opposite side of the main road of the fairy village of Aurora.

Denbo walked across to her as she stood in the doorway of her material and knick knack shop.

"Yes," he said carefully and respectfully. "Is there something I can do for you?"

Mistress Gondola almost smiled. Her lips twitched just slightly. Denbo wasn't known for being polite. In fact he and his friend Raeff were young rascals, and were nearly always in trouble with the older folk of their village.

Aurora village was a small collection of fairy and

elf cottages at the back of Granny Flannigan's property in Northern Queensland, Australia.

Granny loved her heavenly slice of tropical rainforest, and carefully nurtured it. However, she didn't know about the little village. The little people of the village lived happily and comfortably in the secluded spot, glad that they were hidden from the view of humans.

At the moment though, Sylvettia Gondola was a bit concerned.

"I've run out of my beautiful rainbow material that I make from the cobweb of red-back spiders," she told Denbo. "And I was wondering if you and your friend Raeff can go and collect some for me? I know you helped Petula and your mother with that daring adventure with the bird spider," then with a smile and a raised eyebrow she added, "so this should be easy!"

Denbo and Raeff were the best of friends, so Denbo was sure Raeff would be ready and willing to have a little adventure away from the village. Before he had even thought of asking Raeff, he told Mistress

Gondola that they would be delighted. Raeff, after all, often did part time work at the shop lifting some of the heavy rolls of material around, so Denbo thought he wouldn't mind helping him in this little job for her.

When Denbo met Raeff a little later, he was in for quite a surprise. Raeff was furious with him!

"How dare you say I would go without asking me first!" he shouted at Denbo. "I might have been doing something else, you know. You're good at putting me in this type of spot. You did the same thing when Petula broke her wing! And look where that got us!" He took a breath. "Anyway, I DO have other things to do!"

"What exactly?" Denbo asked.

"Things!" Raeff spluttered. "I just have to do things!"

Denbo calmed him down, knowing that this was just a cover up, as Raeff was feeling a little scared. It was because, during their last adventure, they had both got quite a fright when they had found the bird spider and Denbo and Geriron, one of the friends who were with them on that adventure, had got caught in its web. Wally, the Torresian pigeon, had rescued them. Raeff still remembered the whole incident vividly, and told Larimar and Jacoby, the other friends in the group, that he still had nightmares about the whole thing. Petulas' mother had used that web to fix Petulas' wing, so fortunately everything had worked out well in the end.

Petula was his sister, and as far as Denbo was concerned she was back to her usual annoying self.

"Come on, Raeff," he pleaded. "I can't do it without you! It will just be the two of us - you don't have to worry about Lari, Geri and Jac. They are busy helping Mum in the garden at the moment. We won't be away long. You are my best friend and I really want you along. I know you can do this."

Of course, after Denbo had said that, Raeff decided he would go with him. How could he refuse?

They went off in different directions, to let their respective families know what was happening. Then they packed a backpack each with the things they would need, and were soon ready to go.

They set off quickly, before either of them could change their mind. Denbo reassured Raeff that this was going to be an easy task this time.

Unfortunately, Raeff's temper hadn't calmed. He stomped along next to Denbo, frightening the small creatures around them. As soon as they were out of sight of the village, he exploded once again. This time it was over such a small matter.

He stopped in front of Denbo, and put his hands on his hips. Denbo stood still and looked at him warily, wondering what was wrong now.

"And what was the idea of embarrassing me last Tuesday?" Raeff jutted out his chin and looked as if he was ready to punch Denbo.

Denbo screwed up his face in concentration.

"How did I do that?" he asked, still searching in his mind for what he had done.

"You told your Mum, in front of Petula, that I liked

Daisy! How could you!"

"Yes, but you were there too. Petula was busy. I'm sure she didn't take any notice!"

Raeff scowled. "Well, she went and told Daisy!"

"Oh!" Denbo suddenly understood - Raeff more than just liked Daisy. "I'm sorry. I really didn't think that there would be a problem. Please forgive me?"

Raeff made a face and shrugged his shoulders. "Maybe!" he admitted. After all, he didn't think he could stay mad with his best friend for ever. They looked at one another for a few minutes, then Raeff turned and began to walk away.

Denbo spoke very quietly. "Do you know where we have to go?"

Raeff stopped and turned, looking at Denbo with a little sheepish smile on his face.

"Actually?" and he paused for a fraction of a second. "Well, no!"

Denbo reached out his hand and spoke once more.

"Come on, Raeff. Friends?."

Raeff relaxed.

"Of course."

And with that they linked arms and walked off into the bush with something of a swagger. Denbo decided this was the best moment to tell Raeff just what they were going to do.

"What!?" Raeff stopped in mid stride and glared at Denbo. "I know Ruby Redback is a friend - but she hates it when she has to spin more web just for us!"

"I know," answered Denbo. "Perhaps you could think of a way we could get her to help without her losing her temper?"

Raeff snorted. "Yeah, right!"

They walked on some more, Denbo glancing at his friend to see if he was still angry. Raeff seemed lost in thought.

Suddenly he stopped. ‘What if we try a different Redback, instead of Ruby?” he asked Denbo.

“OK,” agreed Denbo. “But who?”

“Isn’t there a colony over by the humans dumping area?”

Denbo wrinkled his nose as he thought.

“Yes, I guess so, but I think that is even more dangerous than asking Ruby! We aren’t supposed to go near there!”

“Well,” Raeff commented. “If we’re going on an adventure, let’s really go on one!”

Denbo nodded his head in agreement.

“I don’t suppose it would hurt to have a back-up supply for Mistress Gondola - then we wouldn’t have to keep asking Ruby and then she wouldn't get so angry." He paused and pursed his lips, stared into the distance for a fraction of a second, then put his hands on his hips, glared at Raeff then grinned.

"I'm making an executive decision! Let's go!"

Raeff grinned back at him.

"OK!" he said and did a little dance on the spot.

Once more they set off. Raeff started to sing, his temper forgotten, and it wasn't long before they were striding vigorously along a small pathway between some tall grass. They linked their arms and began whistling and singing together, not thinking about any dangers that they could encounter.

This was the life!!

ABOUT THE AUTHOR

Maureen Larter was born in England in the late 1940's and came over to Australia when still a toddler. She is a teacher of piano and violin, and lives on the lower Mid North Coast of New South Wales, Australia.

She lives on a small holding of 12 acres, and does her best to live self-sufficiently, while taking care of the soil and the environment. In her spare time she is learning to spin and weave. She has completed and received her certificates in 'Sustainable Agriculture' and 'Comprehensive Writing'. In the past, she has taught English, Social Studies, Music and Mathematics in High Schools within Australia. For a brief period she lived in China teaching English. While there she wrote a textbook for the students of the school.

She still teaches piano and violin.

On wet days, when she can't be out in her garden, and there are no students commandeering her time, she loves to sit and write. She writes children's stories and short stories, as well as occasional articles for magazines.

www.ingramcontent.com/pod-product-compliance
Lightning Source LLC
LaVergne TN
LVHW052253100826
845147LV00001B/33

* 9 7 8 0 9 8 7 3 5 0 0 3 9 *